Meaghan Jette Martin

Gillian Gosman

PowerKiDS press.

New York

Published in 2012 by The Rosen Publishing Group, Inc.
29 East 21st Street, New York, NY 10010

First Edition

Editor: Jennifer Way
Book Design: Kate Laczynski
Layout Design: Julio Gil

Photo Credits: Cover Jeffrey Mayer/WireImage/Getty Images; p. 4 Jon Kopaloff/FilmMagic/Getty Images; p. 7 Kevin Kane/WireImage/Getty Images; p. 8 Bruce Glikas/FilmMagic/Getty Images; p. 11 John Shearer/WireImage/Getty Images; p. 12 Dimitrios Kambouris/WireImage/Getty Images; p. 15 Jamie McCarthy/WireImage/Getty Images; p. 16 Eric Charbonneau/Le Studio/WireImage/Getty Images; p. 19 Gilbert Carrasquillo/WireImage/Getty Images; p. 20 Andy Kropa/Getty Images.

Library of Congress Cataloging-in-Publication Data

Gosman, Gillian.
 Meaghan Jette Martin / by Gillian Gosman. — 1st ed.
     p. cm. — (Kid stars!)
 Includes a webliography and index.
 ISBN 978-1-4488-6192-7 (library binding) — ISBN 978-1-4488-6343-3 (pbk.) —
 ISBN 978-1-4488-6344-0 (6-pack)
 1. Martin, Meaghan, 1992—Juvenile literature. 2. Actors—United States—Juvenile literature. 3. Singers—United States—Juvenile literature. I. Title.
 PN2287.M5215G68 2012
 792.02'8092—dc23
 [B]
                                       2011027670

Manufactured in the United States of America

CPSIA Compliance Information: Batch #WW12PK: For Further Information contact Rosen Publishing, New York, New York at 1-800-237-9932

Contents

Meaghan Martin has played a lot of popular, or "mean" girls. She likes to play dramatic parts to show that she can do lots of different things. Here she is at an event in 2010.

Meet Meaghan Martin

Meaghan Jette Martin remembers the days when she had braces on her teeth and glasses slipping down her nose, but those days are long gone. These days, you will find her in movies and on television playing the part of the prettiest girl in school.

This book will show you that Martin is more than a pretty face. She has played mean girls but makes videos that remind kids that in real life, bullying is hurtful and wrong. She has done comedy, crime dramas, and small, artistic films. If you do not think that is enough, she also sings and dances!

The Early Years

Meaghan was born on February 17, 1992. She has a sister, Rebecca, and two brothers, Zachary and Sean. They grew up in the desert city of Las Vegas, Nevada. Meaghan says that while she and her siblings did not always get along as kids, as they have gotten older they have become closer.

Meaghan began modeling at age five. Her first modeling job was in a fashion show for Disney clothing. She also appeared in television **advertisements** for toys such as Barbie and Cabbage Patch Kids. These humble, or simple, beginnings, gave Meaghan a taste of the life she wanted. It was the beginning of a career in show business!

In 2010, Martin was one of the stars at Pop-Con.
This was a festival of young pop stars and actors.

Martin has a lifelong interest in the theater. Here she is with Jordin Sparks in 2010, after Sparks's performance in the Broadway musical *In the Heights*.

Meaghan loved the spotlight, and it was not long before she realized she was meant to be a star. One of her heroes growing up was the actress Sarah Michelle Gellar. Gellar started acting at a young age and became famous as the star of the TV show *Buffy the Vampire Slayer*. Meaghan began her acting career in **community theater** in Las Vegas.

After she finished ninth grade, she decided to be homeschooled. This way she would have the time and freedom to act more. Not long after, she moved to Los Angeles, California, and earned her first role in a **professional** theater production. The show was Jason Robert Brown's musical about being a teen, *13*.

Making It on TV!

Meaghan's big break came in 2006. That year, she appeared in a pilot for the television show *Cooking Rocks*! The show did not get picked up, but Meaghan's television career soon took off.

In 2007, Meaghan got a role on an **episode** of the Nickelodeon **sitcom** *Just Jordan*. Then she appeared on an episode of the CBS crime drama *Close to Home* and on Disney's comedy *The Suite Life of Zack and Cody*. Finally, in 2008, she was chosen to play the part of Tess Tyler in the Disney television movie *Camp Rock*. This would be her breakthrough role.

Doing lots of one-episode roles helped Meaghan get noticed and be chosen for *Camp Rock*. Here is Meaghan in 2009 at the opening of *The Twilight Saga: New Moon*.

Here is the cast of *Camp Rock*. From left to right are Anna Maria Perez de Tagle, Kevin Jonas, Meaghan, Joe Jonas, Demi Lovato, and Nick Jonas.

Spending the Summer at Camp Rock

Camp Rock had an all-star cast of Disney teen favorites. Demi Lovato played Mitchie Torres, a hardworking girl who dreams of being a singer. Joe, Kevin, and Nick Jonas play the members of boy band Connect 3. Meaghan plays the mean girl, Tess Tyler. Tess is not a nice person, but she is fun to watch! This movie was Meaghan's biggest role yet. It gave her a chance to show off her singing, dancing, and acting to a larger audience.

Critics praised Meaghan's performance. *TV Guide* chose Meaghan as one of the "13 Hottest Young Stars to Watch" in 2008. The movie was hugely popular.

Rock On!

In 2010, Martin took on the role of Tess Tyler once again in the *Camp Rock* **sequel**. It was called *Camp Rock 2: The Final Jam*. This time, a new camp called Camp Star opened up across the lake from Camp Rock. Tess has joined the campers and staff at the new camp. Once again, there are fun performances by the Camp Rock and Camp Star kids. There is a contest in which the future of Camp Rock is at stake.

Martin played a supporting role in the *Camp Rock* movies. A supporting role is not as big a part as a lead role, but it lets an actor show off her unique talents. In Martin's case, it also helped her get noticed for leading roles!

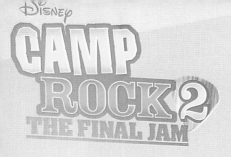

Camp Rock 2: The Final Jam aired on the Disney Channel on September 3, 2010. It premiered, or was first played, at a New York movie theater about two weeks before that. Here is Martin at that premiere.

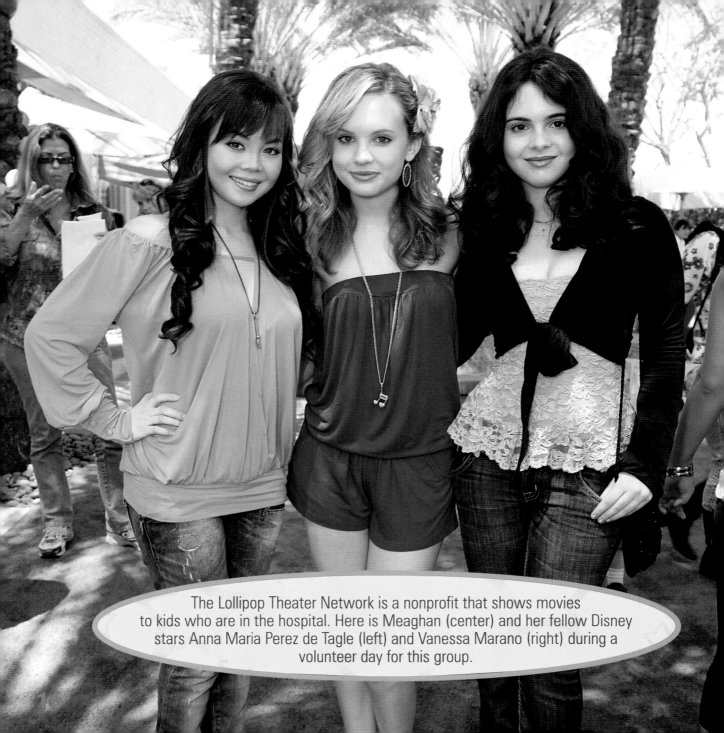

The Lollipop Theater Network is a nonprofit that shows movies to kids who are in the hospital. Here is Meaghan (center) and her fellow Disney stars Anna Maria Perez de Tagle (left) and Vanessa Marano (right) during a volunteer day for this group.

Television Star

In 2009, Meaghan landed a role on the ABC Family sitcom *10 Things I Hate About You*. The show was based on the 1999 movie of the same name. On the sitcom, Meaghan played Bianca Stratford, the younger of two sisters. The sisters were different, but together they got through the ups and downs of high-school life. Martin has said that her relationship with her sister helped her prepare for playing Bianca. This show lasted for two seasons and ended in 2010.

In 2011, Martin had a starring role in *Mean Girls 2*, playing Johanna Mitchell. *Mean Girls 2* was a television movie sequel to the 2004 movie *Mean Girls*. This TV movie was a hit with young viewers!

Acting is not Martin's only passion. She also enjoys singing. For the *Camp Rock* **sound track**, she recorded three songs. They are called "Too Cool," "2 Stars," and "We Rock." For the sequel's sound track, she recorded "Walkin' in My Shoes," "Tear It Down," and "It's On." Meaghan also sang on one of the *DisneyMania* albums, singing the Disney song "When You Wish upon a Star."

Martin also enjoys making and posting videos. She has her own YouTube channel where she posts videos she has made and videos she wants to share.

Meaghan also recorded a song for the *Wizards of Waverly Place* sound track. It was a cover of Olivia Newton-John's song "Magic."

Martin has worked with other charities besides Autism Speaks and Broadway Cares/Equity Fights AIDS. She has also helped collect toys for a charity called Toys for Tots, shown here.

Meaghan in Real Life

Martin believes in using her fame to draw awareness to issues that matter to her. One of her brothers has **Asperger's syndrome**. Asperger's syndrome is an **autism spectrum disorder**. It causes problems with how the brain takes in and understands information.

Martin works for the **charity** Autism Speaks to raise awareness of autism. She also **volunteers** with the City of Hope cancer research center and is active in the fight for AIDS awareness through the group Broadway Cares/Equity Fights AIDS.

FUN FACTS

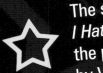 The sitcom and movie *10 Things I Hate About You* were based on the play *The Taming of the Shrew* by William Shakespeare.

 Meaghan also appeared in the small movie *Dear Lemon Lima*, which came out in theaters in 2009.

 When it aired on ABC Family, *Mean Girls 2* was the number-one television movie of the week for viewers between the ages of 12 and 34.

 Martin studied ballet, tap, and hip-hop dance.

 Martin loves the Harry Potter books!

 Meaghan's audition, or tryout, for *Camp Rock* lasted 8 hours!

 Between 2007 and 2010, Meaghan was the voice of Naminé in the video game *Kingdom Hearts*.

 The *Camp Rock* sound track sold more than 1 million copies. The sequel's sound track sold more than 500,000 copies.

 Meaghan appears in the music video for Demi Lovato's hit 2009 song "Remember December."

 Martin collects snow globes.

Glossary

advertisements (ad-vur-TYZ-ments) Public notices that tell people about products, events, or things a person needs.

Asperger's syndrome (AHS-per-gerz SIN-drohm) A disorder in which people have trouble relating to other people and with certain other activities.

autism spectrum disorder (AW-tih-zum SPEK-trum dis-AWR-der) A disorder in which people have trouble dealing with others or talking.

charity (CHER-uh-tee) A group that gives help to the needy.

community theater (kuh-MYOO-nih-tee THEE-eh-ter) Theater produced by and for a community.

episode (EH-puh-sohd) One part of a TV series.

professional (pruh-FESH-nul) Being paid for what one does.

sequel (SEE-kwel) The next in a series.

sitcom (SIT-kom) A funny TV show that is usually about things that happen in everyday life.

sound track (SOWND TRAK) The music in a movie.

volunteers (vah-lun-TEERZ) Offers to work for no money.

Index

B
brothers, 6, 21

C
career, 6, 9, 10
comedy, 5, 10
community theater, 9

D
drama(s), 5, 10

F
films, 5

J
job, 6

L
Las Vegas, Nevada,
   6, 9
Los Angeles,
   California, 9

M
movie(s), 5, 10, 13,
   17, 22
musical, 9

R
role, 9–10, 13, 14, 17

S
school, 5
sister(s), 6, 17

Web Sites

Due to the changing nature of Internet links, PowerKids Press
has developed an online list of Web sites related to the subject
of this book. This site is updated regularly. Please use this link
to access the list:
www.powerkidslinks.com/kids/martin/